This Little Tiger book belongs to:

_____

_____

_____

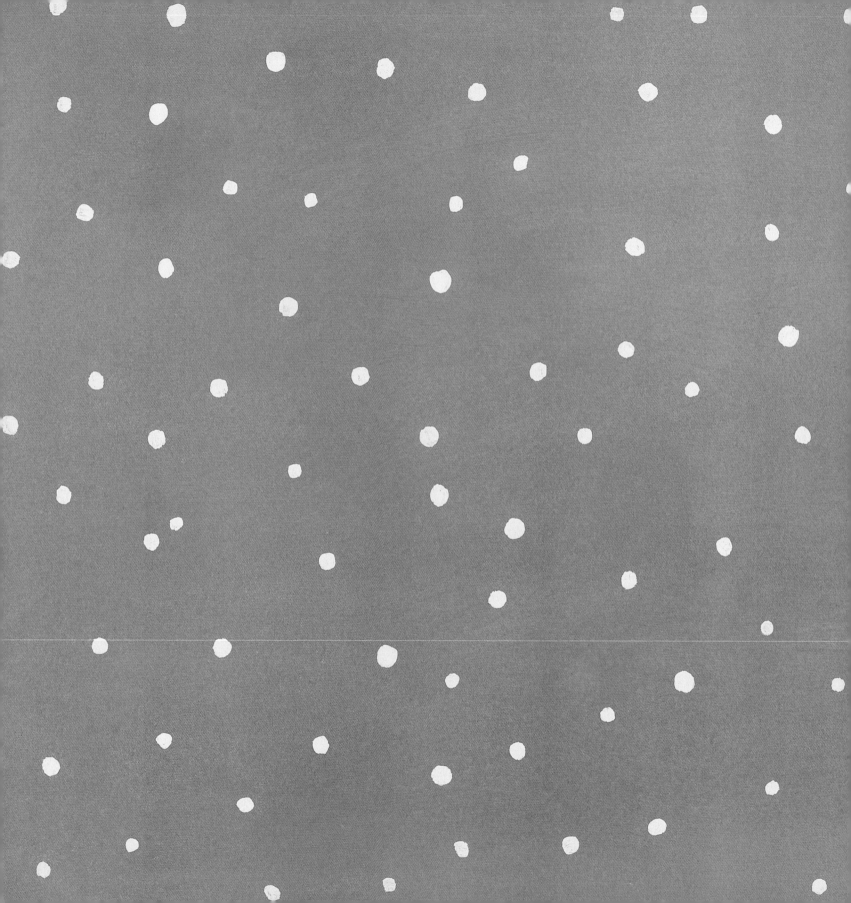

For
Noah x

LITTLE TIGER PRESS
1 The Coda Centre, 189 Munster Road,
London SW6 6AW
First published in Great Britain 2001
This edition published 2001
Text and illustrations
copyright © Tim Warnes 2001
Tim Warnes has asserted his right
to be identified as the author
and illustrator of this work under the
Copyright, Designs and Patents Act, 1988
A CIP catalogue record for this book is available
from the British Library

Printed in China

4 6 8 10 9 7 5 3

Can't you sleep, Dotty?

Tim Warnes

LITTLE TIGER PRESS
London

Dotty couldn't sleep.
It was her first night
in her new home.

She tried sleeping
upside down.

She tried
snuggling up
to Penguin.

She even tried
lying on the
floor.

AWOOOOOOOOOOooooo

But still Dotty
couldn't sleep.

Dotty's howling woke up Pip the mouse. "Can't you sleep, Dotty?" he asked. "Perhaps you should try counting the stars like I do."

But Dotty could only count up to one. *That* wasn't enough to send her to sleep.

What could she do next?

AWOOOOOOOOOO

Susie the bird was awake now. "Can't you sleep, Dotty?" she twittered. "I always have a little drink before I go to bed."

Dotty went to her bowl and
had a little drink.

But then she made
a little puddle.
Well *that*
didn't help!
What *could* Dotty
do to get to sleep?

AWOOOOOOOOO..

Whiskers the rabbit had woken up, too.
"Can't you sleep, Dotty?" he mumbled
sleepily. "I hide away in my burrow
at bedtime. That always works."

Dotty dived under her blanket so that
only her bottom was showing. But it was
all dark under there with no light at all.

Dotty was too scared to go to sleep.

Tommy the tortoise
poked his head from
out of his shell.

"Can't you sleep, Dotty?" he sighed. "I like
to sleep where it's bright and sunny."

Dotty liked that idea . . .

. . . and turned on her torch!

"Turn it off, Dotty!"
shouted all her friends.
"*We* can't get to sleep now!"

Poor Dotty was too
tired to try anything else.
Then Tommy had a great idea . . .

He helped Dotty into her bed.

What Dotty needed for the first

night in her new home was . . .

. . . to snuggle up among *all* her new friends. Soon they were all fast asleep.

Night night, Dotty!

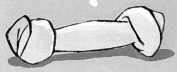

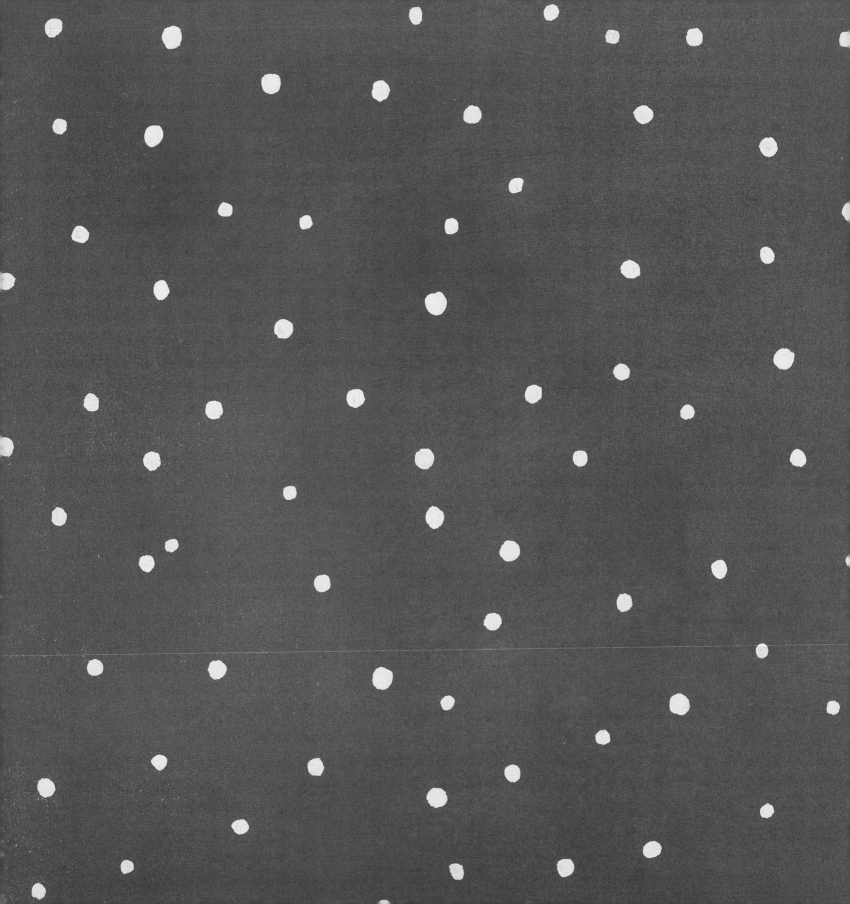